For Sarah, who
introduced me
to Eric

ERIC THE RED
A Bodley Head Book: 0 370 32626 1

First published in Great Britain in 2003 by
The Bodley Head, an imprint of
Random House Children's Books

1 3 5 7 9 10 8 6 4 2

Copyright © Caroline Glicksman 2003

The right of Caroline Glicksman to be identified as the
author and illustrator of this work has been
asserted in accordance with the Copyright, Designs
and Patents Act, 1988.

RANDOM HOUSE CHILDREN'S BOOKS
61–63 Uxbridge Rd, London W5 5SA
A division of The Random House Group Ltd

RANDOM HOUSE AUSTRALIA (PTY) LTD
20 Alfred Street, Milsons Point, Sydney,
New South Wales 2061, Australia

RANDOM HOUSE NEW ZEALAND LTD
18 Poland Road, Glenfield, Auckland 10, New Zealand

RANDOM HOUSE (PTY) LTD
Endulini, 5A Jubilee Road,
Parktown 2193,
South Africa

THE RANDOM HOUSE GROUP
Limited Reg. No. 954009
www.kidsatrandomhouse.co.uk

A CIP catalogue record for this
book is available from the
British Library.

Printed and bound
in Malaysia

Eric the Red

Caroline Glicksman

THE
BODLEY HEAD
LONDON

Eric is a very unusual bear.

Most bears are brown or black or white.

For one thing, Eric is red.

Very red.

So red that he glows
in the dark.

And Eric is very, very clever, especially with numbers.

He even dreams
about numbers!

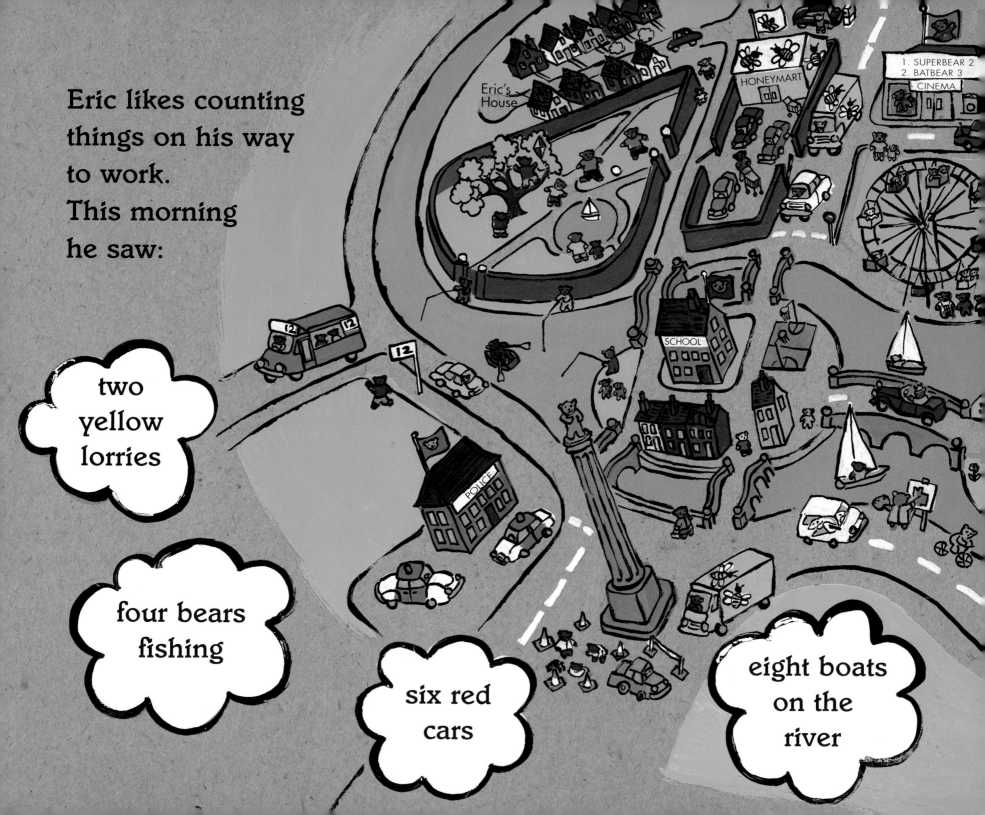

Eric likes counting
things on his way
to work.
This morning
he saw:

two
yellow
lorries

four bears
fishing

six red
cars

eight boats
on the
river

Eric has a very important job at the Big Bear Bank.

Every day, he counts up
all the bank's money and
puts it in the big safe.

Then he thinks up a
new set of numbers for
the lock and closes
the safe tight.

Eric is the only bear
who knows the numbers!

Every so often, Eric helps at the front counter of the bank. He doesn't like working there because sometimes badly behaved bears laugh at his red fur.

Then Eric wishes he was at home, eating lots of honey, and doing bigger and bigger sums on his computer.

VROOM!

Just then an ice-cream van burst
through the door of the bank
and two polar bears jumped
out. Erica gasped.

Without thinking, he growled at the first polar bear.

The polar bear was so surprised that he stepped back, slipped on an ice lolly, and banged his head on the floor.

In a flash, the second polar bear grabbed Erica, jumped over the glass screen, and spun Eric round on his chair. Fast.

"TELL ME THE NUMBERS TO OPEN THE SAFE, TOMATO FACE!" he shouted.

"YOU'VE GOT FIVE SECONDS!" shouted the polar bear.
"FIVE!

FOUR!!

THREE!!!

TWO!!!!"

"Wait!" gasped Eric.
"That's it! TWO!
The two times table! The numbers
I saw this morning. Two . . . four . . ."

The polar bear dropped Erica
and started turning
the lock on the safe.

"Six . . . eight . . . ten . . ."
continued Eric, but
his head was spinning
so much that
he couldn't remember
the last number.

"**TWELVE . . .**" said Erica. Suddenly, the safe opened and the polar bear started grabbing the money as fast as he could. Soon he was right inside the safe.

Eric's head stopped spinning.

He helped Erica to her feet and . . .

Wah! Wah! Wah!
Five police bears rushed in and
arrested the first polar bear, who
was still lying dazed on the floor.

"You caught them red-handed!" said Erica. She gave Eric's paw a gentle squeeze.

"I couldn't have done it alone," said Eric. Suddenly, he noticed . . .

. . . the maths book that Erica
was holding in her paws.
"You like maths too!" he said.
"I've never met another bear
who liked numbers," said Erica.

Eric glowed very red.

"Wouldn't it be fun to do sums
together?" said Erica.
Eric grinned. "Yes, twice as
much fun!" he said.

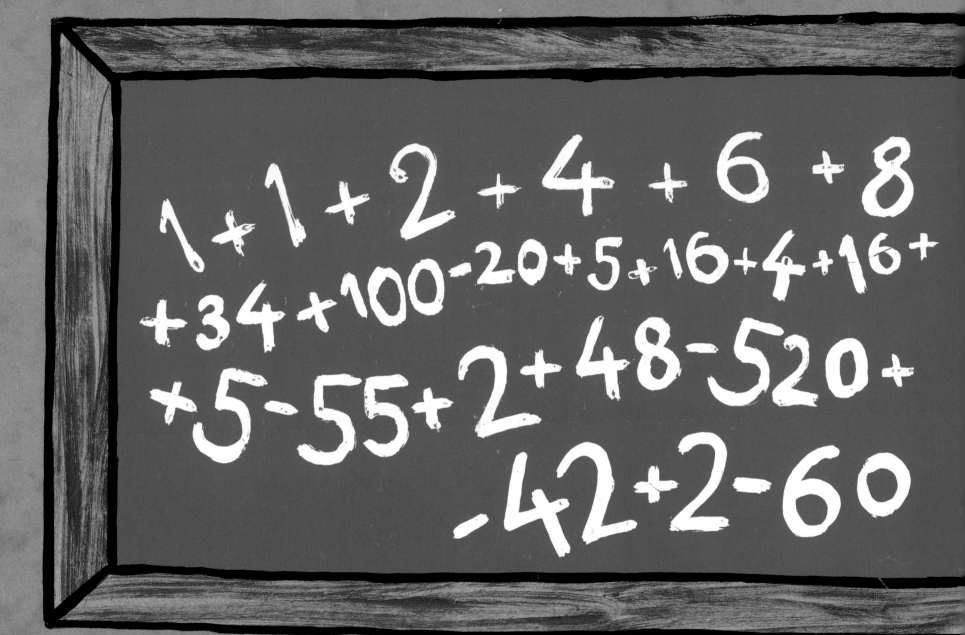

$1 + 1 + 2 + 4 + 6 + 8$
$+ 34 + 100 - 20 + 5 + 16 + 4 + 16 +$
$+ 5 - 55 + 2 + 48 - 520 +$
$- 42 + 2 - 60$